C0-DUO-122

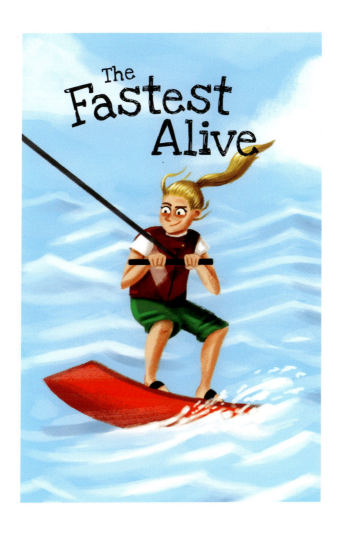

The Fastest Alive

By Elise Wallace
Illustrated by Dan Widdowson

Publishing Credits

Rachelle Cracchiolo, M.S.Ed., *Publisher*
Conni Medina, M.A.Ed., *Editor in Chief*
Nika Fabienke, Ed.D., *Content Director*
Véronique Bos, *Creative Director*
Shaun N. Bernadou, *Art Director*
Carol Huey-Gatewood, M.A.Ed., *Editor*
Valerie Morales, *Associate Editor*
Kevin Pham, *Graphic Designer*

Image Credits

Illustrated by Dan Widdowson

5301 Oceanus Drive
Huntington Beach, CA 92649-1030
www.tcmpub.com
ISBN 978-1-6449-1327-7
© 2020 Teacher Created Materials, Inc.

Table of Contents

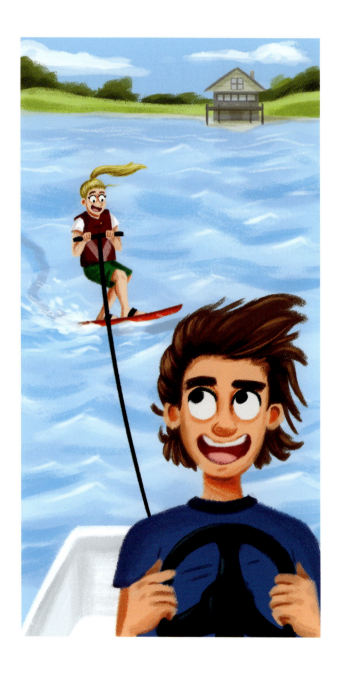

CHAPTER ONE

Never Fast Enough

It's early morning, and we're completely alone. The surface of the lake is still, and the surrounding forest is strangely quiet. By the afternoon, the lake will be overrun with tourists, but at 5:00 a.m., everyone is still sleeping. Well, everyone but me and Kit, my driver.

"Skis are on!" I give Kit an enthusiastic thumbs-up.

Kit grins and starts the boat. I veer left and right, creating gigantic waves. Then, I start wake jumping, catching more air each time. I want to go higher, farther, and faster.

"Kit, you're not going fast enough!" I shout into the wind.

Kit shakes his head but hits the gas. We're flying across the lake, and I can feel the wind and water working with me, pushing and pulling when I need them to. We go faster, and I get a familiar pull in the pit of my stomach. It's how I feel when I'm utterly terrified. It's my very favorite feeling.

CHAPTER TWO

Brave from the Beginning

I grew up in Texas in the 1950s and 1960s. Most of my childhood was spent outdoors. Ever since I was little, I've been climbing up one thing and jumping off another. I was always getting into trouble with my older brother, Charlie. Just like me, Charlie loved mischief and adventure.

My parents weren't too bothered by my wild streak. But the neighbors were another story. According to them, and just about everyone else, I didn't act like a girl was supposed to. Or at least, how people used to think a girl should act.

When I got a bit older, I heard the same thing from my teachers and classmates. Looking back, I can't help but feel as though I was born at the wrong time. How much easier would it have been to be born today? Now, it is much more accepted for girls to be thrill-seekers.

My brother and I were always having competitions. We would compete to see who could run the fastest, swim the farthest, and climb the highest. For the longest time, he beat me at everything. But that changed when I was 11 and he was 12.

Growing up, my brother and I had a gigantic oak tree in the backyard. Charlie and I would take turns climbing the tree, seeing who could go the

highest. I'll never forget the first time I beat him.

The memory is so clear. I'm halfway up the tree, and my legs are trembling. I'm terrified, but I keep pulling myself up, one branch at a time. I don't stop until I'm almost to the top of the giant oak.

I look down at my brother. Even from way up high, I can see his grin. That's when Charlie started calling me Wild One. From that day on, my stunts only got crazier.

I don't recommend most of the stunts I tried when I was younger. They were all dangerous. When you're a kid, you think you're invincible—that nothing can touch you. But now that I'm an adult, I have the aches and pains to prove I wasn't.

One of the scariest things I tried was jumping off the roof onto a trampoline. I know, not smart. I made it to the trampoline but then was launched onto our cement patio. I broke seven bones in my right leg. My parents wouldn't let me out of the house for three months. Charlie made fun of me for a long time.

Some of my favorite childhood memories are of go-karting. As soon as I was old enough to drive a real car, I began racing locally. I was the youngest person at the racetrack, and I was also the only girl. Everyone thought I was crazy until I started winning.

CHAPTER THREE

My First Race

I'll never forget the first time I raced competitively. I was 20 years old and had been practically living at the racetrack. I knew my car inside and out, and my times were getting better every day.

It took me a while to summon the courage to enter my first race. I was afraid of what people would say. I was even afraid that they wouldn't let me race because I was a girl. In the end, I'm so thankful I pushed past my fears. I wouldn't be where I am today if I hadn't.

My whole family came to watch me race. I can still see Charlie in the stands, jumping up and down. He had a sign that said *Wild One 4 the Win!* Having their support meant everything to me, and even though I placed fifth in the race, the day felt like a win.

Most of the racers didn't talk to me before or after the race. But there was one racer who ran up to me once the race was over. This was Kit!

I remember being scared about what he was going to say. When I first saw Kit, I thought he was just another boy who was going to give me a hard time about racing. I was especially worried because he was the only person I'd beat in the race—I had come in fifth place, and Kit had come in sixth.

Thankfully, Kit had come to congratulate me! He had heard that it was my first race in a competition. Kit teased that he was feeling a bit under the weather but would beat me next time. It was the first time I was accepted by one of my peers, and it felt fantastic. Even though we'd just met, I knew Kit and I would be friends for a very long time.

CHAPTER FOUR

Fast, Faster, Fastest

I kept racing and got better and better. Kit and I practiced together every day. We pushed each other to beat our best times. I even got Mary, one of my best friends from high school, to try racing with us. This was one of the happiest times of my life. I had a small group of friends who understood my passion for adventure and cheered me on at every race.

As time passed, I entered bigger and bigger races. Sometimes I won, sometimes I lost, but I was almost always the only woman competing.

With time, I even got a little bored of racing! It felt too easy. I wanted to do things no one had done before. I wanted to break world records, to become the fastest person on the planet.

At that point, the fastest I'd ever gone was close to 200 miles per hour. I wanted to find a way to go faster. Kit and I asked around until we found a designer who was building a new kind of car.

It was love at first sight when I saw The Reckless, a three-wheeled rocket car. The car's designer, Hank, told me that the car was built to break 500 miles per hour. I wanted to jump in the driver's seat right then.

I set my first world record behind the wheel of The Reckless, I was 25 years old. I'd broken 500 miles per hour and become the fastest person on land. Setting this record felt like the biggest thing that would ever happen to me, but boy, was I wrong! Some of my biggest achievements were still to come.

CHAPTER FIVE

Lights, Camera, Leap!

A lot changed after I set the land speed record. News stations had covered the event. It felt like I was mildly famous. People began to recognize me when I was out of the house. Every once in a while, someone would ask me for an autograph. The new attention felt strange, but I have to admit that I liked it.

Setting a world record also provided me with new opportunities. A few weeks after I set the world record, I got a call from an agent. He wanted to book me as a stuntwoman on a TV show.

Before the call, I'd never heard of a stuntwoman. I had heard of Hollywood stunt people, but had assumed they were all men. As it turns out, I was sort of right. When I first started working in Hollywood, stuntwomen were few and far between.

My first big job was on a show called *Girl from Space.* The show was about an alien girl named Ingo who had superpowers. Many people called Ingo the female version of Superman. She had super speed and super strength, and could fly, too.

Every episode presented new challenges. Ingo was always getting into trouble, which meant *I* was always getting into trouble. During my time on the show, I did a ton of stunts. I leapt from 10-story buildings. I flipped cars into brick walls. I barreled through fire.

Despite the excitement of the show, this time of my life was pretty unhappy. I didn't get much respect from my peers, even though I was often risking my life during filming. But even in the low times, I tried to keep my head up. I focused on the work. I wanted to be the best stunt person in Hollywood. As my years in Hollywood continued, more women began working as stunt performers. It was great! I had female friends who understood my career and shared my passion. But life wasn't perfect. We were getting big jobs in film, but we still struggled to be accepted by the film industry as true stunt performers.

For most of my career, it felt like I was trying to prove something. I wanted to prove that women are brave.

I wanted to prove that we are worthy of recognition and proper pay. I don't know if I accomplished this. But I do think I helped stuntwomen become more respected in the film business.

I worked as a stuntwoman for a little over a decade. I worked on many shows and films. But as the years passed, it began to feel like it was time to move on. I wanted to get back to my first love: setting records.

CHAPTER SIX

My Greatest Stunt

Kit and I started working together again. I had missed my old friend! In the coming years, Kit would help me train for a bunch of records. We trained on both land and water. I had two main goals: I wanted to become the fastest motorcyclist and the fastest water skier.

I was able to meet some of my goals but not others. Motorcycles and I, it turns out, do not mix. I never felt comfortable on a motorcycle, and I definitely never came close to breaking a speed record. However, with Kit's help, I did break another record. I became the fastest woman on water skis!

I've often been asked what I think was my greatest stunt. It's a difficult question to answer. I've had many thrilling experiences. But if I had to name one stunt, it would be when I jumped out of a plane without a parachute.

Though you wouldn't know it, I'm afraid of heights. Even when I climbed trees as a child, I was always scared to look down. When I got the opportunity to jump from a plane, I hesitated. Then, my thrill-seeking spirit kicked in. I was totally game.

I'd done aerial stunts while I was working on *Girl from Space*. I'd

jumped from buildings with only an airbag to catch me. You have to stay focused when you make a jump, which is difficult because the natural reaction is to freak out. But if you don't focus on where you're landing, you could easily end up in the hospital or worse.

So, when I made the jump, I knew I had to stay utterly calm. We were 200 feet up, and I could barely see the airbag. I honestly thought I might die. But I made the jump and set the record for the highest fall without a parachute. I never wanted to do it again!

CHAPTER SEVEN

Wild Ones

Being a professional daredevil was filled with challenges. Some of those challenges were part of the job. But others were unnecessary. I should have been shown more respect by my peers. Instead, I was often treated unfairly because I was a female. Still, I couldn't have had any other life. My passion for danger required action.

In some ways, I count myself very lucky. I had friends who believed in me. I also had the support of my family. This gave me the confidence to pursue my dreams even when things got tough.

It took many years, but eventually stuntwomen became respected in the film world. I know that my work and the work of other stuntwomen were important. Because of our work, young girls will have an easier path to their dreams. For this, I'm grateful. I can't wait to see what the next generation of wild ones will do. I will be cheering them on!

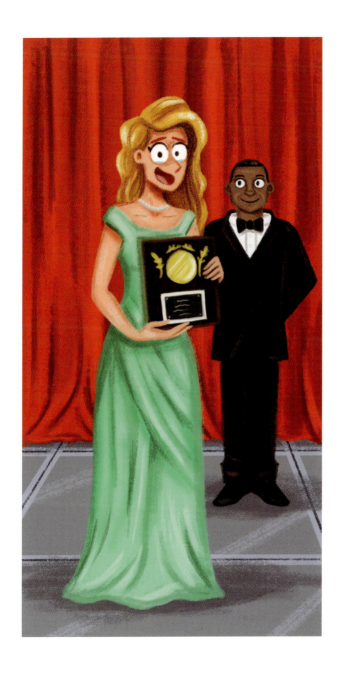

About Us

The Author

Elise Wallace is definitely not a daredevil. She prefers stationary, indoor activities such as reading, writing, and watching movies. Some of these books and movies *do* feature daredevils. In Wallace's opinion, the best way to experience danger is at a distance! Wallace's favorite thrill-seeker is Kitty O'Neil. She was a former stuntwoman for Wonder Woman. O'Neil was one of the main inspirations for this book!

The Illustrator

Dan Widdowson is a children's illustrator from England. He graduated from an arts university and has been working on children's illustration projects ever since. With a keen interest in storytelling and narrative, he is working to bring his own picture books to life soon.